# IF THIS BIRD HAD POCKETS

## A Poem in Your Pocket Day Celebration

Poems by **Amy Ludwig VanDerwater**

Illustrations by **Emma J. Virján**

WORD*SONG*

AN IMPRINT OF ASTRA BOOKS FOR YOUNG READERS

*New York*

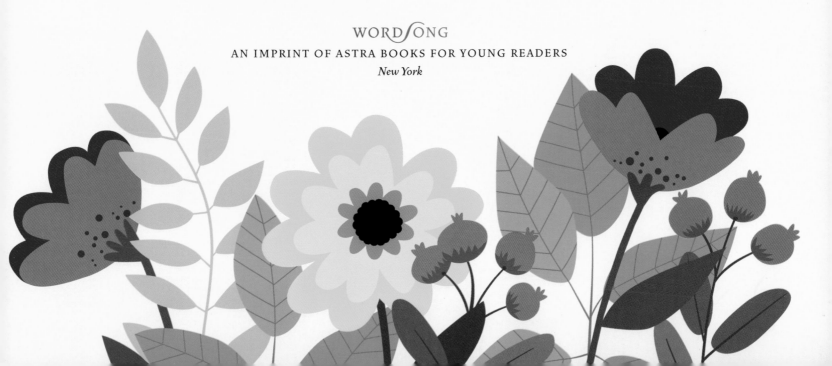

In 2002, Poem in Your Pocket Day was introduced in New York City
by the Office of the Mayor and the city's Department of Cultural Affairs
and Education. In 2008, The Academy of American Poets
brought the holiday to the entire United States,
and in 2016, the League of Canadian Poets further
expanded it to Canada. Both countries celebrate
National Poetry Month in April.

Poem in Your Pocket Day invites everyone to carry and share poems
and is celebrated on a different April day each year.
But of course, we may choose to carry poems and celebrate
Poem in Your Pocket Day on any day or every day.
How magical it would be if animals carried poems too . . .

# Contents

## Poem in Your Pocket Day
*by Me*

Tomorrow I will carry
a poem in my pocket.
Today I need to find or write
the perfect one for me.

As I seek a poem,
I peek out of my window.
I spy a smallish bird
perching in a tallish tree.

And I wonder—

If this bird had pockets,
if this bird could write,
would it scribble poems about
Nectar?
Humming?
Flight?

So suddenly I'm thinking
about creatures everywhere.
Which poems would they carry?
Which poems would they share?

# Sipping Song
### by Ruby-Throated Hummingbird

My feathers
are tiny.
I sing
with my wings.

I'm ruby.
I'm emerald.
I shine
like a locket.

You'll discover
I hover
near flowers
for hours.

I find
nectar poems
in hollyhock pockets.

# Growing Up
### *by Eastern Newt*

I begin in water—
one wee spring egg.

I swim as a larva—
growing leg after leg.

I crawl through my forest—
a red and spotted eft.

I return to water.
It's as if I never left.

# Rarely a Birdeater
*by Goliath Birdeater*

I'm a gargantuan tarantula.

From my name
you might assume
I dine on birds
but birds can fly.

I cannot fly, so I consume
lizards
invertebrates
amphibians
mice
(yes, a small bird will suffice).

I sink my fangs.
They liquify.
I suck them down
like lemonade.

*Snatch.*
*Slurp.*
Goodbye.

# We Farm Fungus
### by Leafcutter Ant

We carry many times our weight.
Our colony's humongous.

We cut and carry leaves all day.
We bring them to our fungus.

Here
beneath green parasols
we know one thing is true—

*if you feed your fungus,*
*your fungus will feed you.*

# My Name
## by Bottlenose Dolphin

The sound of my clicks
helps me see in the sea.
I send out my clicks
and they bounce
back to me.

I buzz. I whistle.
I creak. I squeak.
Dolphins are clever.
Dolphins can speak.

My pod
provides protection
on the hunt
or in a game.
When I get lost
my podmates call.

I recognize my name.

# Bath Time
### by Short-Tailed Chinchilla

I take my bath without a splash.
I wash in old volcanic ash.

To look and feel my best I must
spin and twist in ancient dust.

Dusty, fluffy, dense, and fine—
no fur on earth is soft as mine.

# Think Fingerprints
### by Northern Giraffe

I am not a combination
of a leopard and a camel.
I mostly stand.
I hardly sleep.
I am the tallest mammal.

Most girl giraffes live in a herd.
This is my newest daughter.
We munch so many leaves
because
it's hard to bend for water.

Look closely at my girl and me
from spot to spot to spot.
Do you think we look the same?
Look closer.
We do not.

My pattern is unique to me.
Hers unique to her.
Think fingerprints—
one of a kind.
Know me by my fur.

## Metaphor in a Meadow
### by *Spotted Turtle*

My old shell is sprinkled
with golden constellations.
I am a walking sky.

# Tail of Red, Tip of White
## *by Red Fox*

In forest
ever brown and green,
I am a splendid spark.

My poem is
my fiery tail
flashing in the dark.

# Wilderness and Safety
### by Barren-Ground Caribou

If you've never
carried antlers
on your head,

if you've never
slept in whipping winds
upon a frozen bed,

if you've never
dug for lichen
in glittering snow,

then you've never
been a caribou,
so you will never know

the wilderness of winter
or the safety of a herd.

It is grand to be a caribou.
Take my word.

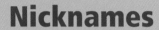

# Nicknames
### *by Bluegill*

My nicknames
are a poem.
(Copperbelly)

I feed and grow
and swim.
(Brim)

I like
a quiet river.
(Sunny)

By any name
I gleam.
(Bream)

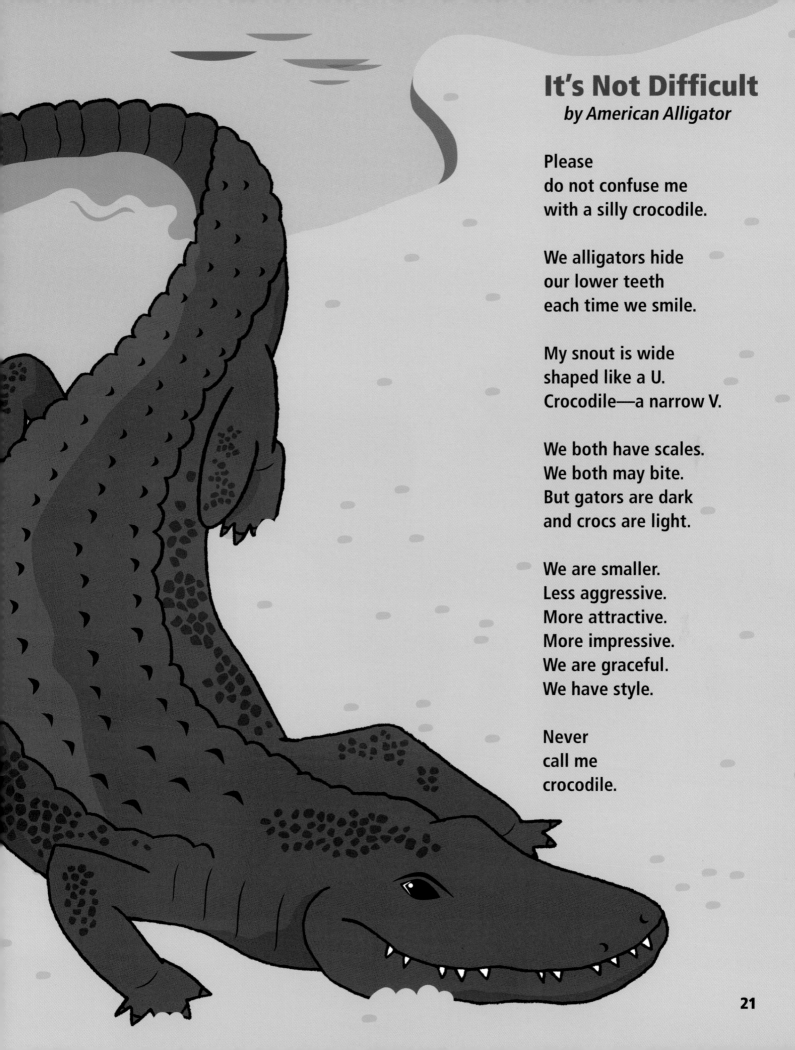

# It's Not Difficult
*by American Alligator*

Please
do not confuse me
with a silly crocodile.

We alligators hide
our lower teeth
each time we smile.

My snout is wide
shaped like a U.
Crocodile—a narrow V.

We both have scales.
We both may bite.
But gators are dark
and crocs are light.

We are smaller.
Less aggressive.
More attractive.
More impressive.
We are graceful.
We have style.

Never
call me
crocodile.

# Meanings
### by Gray Wolf

Do you hear our howls at night?
Are you filled with awe and fright?

Do our howls haunt you in dreams?
Do you wonder what they mean?

If one wanders from our pack,
    we will howl to bring her back.

If a pack invades our land,
    we will howl to take a stand.

We howl to each other—
*We are family.*
*We found prey.*

Powerful.
Magnificent.
We have a lot to say.

*Aroooooooooooooooooooooooooo!*

# Something to Appreciate
### by Royal Starfish

When stars are wounded,
we create.
This is our legendary trait.

Allow me to elaborate.

If predators should amputate
my arm or four, I'll calmly wait
for each one will regenerate
(within a year, at any rate).

We've no need to exaggerate
congratulate or celebrate.
The truth is simple.

Stars are great.

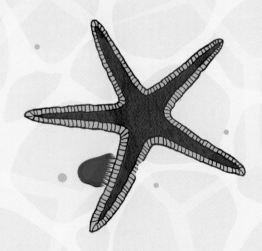

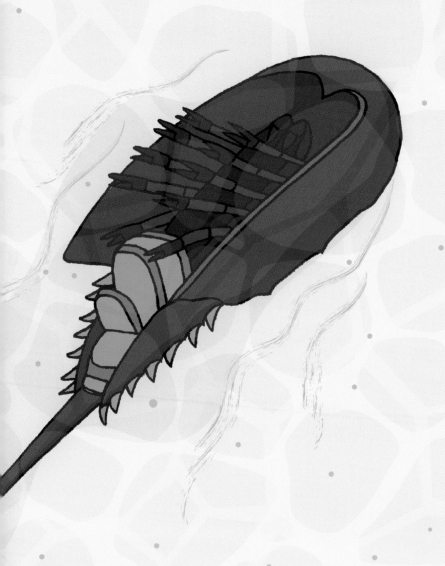

## An Old Story
### by Atlantic Horseshoe Crab

We're ancient, patient
horseshoe crabs.
We predate dinosaurs.
We've lived *soooo* long.

We dig. We swim.
Our blood is blue.
We molt our shells.
We crabs are strong.

Our ancestors
are ocean history.
We are part understood.
Part mystery.

Our flap-like gills
look like book pages.
Our story lives
throughout the ages.

Year by year
one thing is clear.
Egg by egg
we persevere.

# Dear Milkweed
### *by Monarch Butterfly*

As an egg
I stuck to your leaf.
When I hatched
I ate it.

As a caterpillar
I ate more,
        more,
            more.

And now I float
        flower to flower
hour by hour
        sipping your nectar
laying my eggs.

I have wings now.
I can soar.
You knew me before.

Thank you.

# Instinct
## by Star-Nosed Mole

A star-nosed mole cannot control
this need to dig an endless hole.
I feel it in my furry soul.
*Tunnel. Tunnel.* That's my role.

My two small eyes can barely see
but no one has a nose like me.
I swim and dig and touch and kill.
I always have. I always will.

27

# Secret Pocket
### by Sea Otter

I sport
a secret pocket
where I store
my special rock.

It is good
for smashing mussels
on my
fluffy otter tummy.

My rock
is like a charm,
which I keep
beneath my arm.

Excuse me
for a moment.
*CRACK!*
S-w-a-l-l-o-w.

That was yummy.

# My Poem
### *by Me*

Each creature
lives a poem
without ever
writing a line.

I am a creature too.

I write.
This poem is mine.

I imagine,
         read about,
                 dream of
life in the
wondrous wild.

I love to learn
about animals

I am an animal child.

For teachers, with admiration —*ALV*

For my friend, Patrice Barton —*EJV*

**Acknowledgment:**
The publisher thanks Linda Zajac for her careful review of the text and illustrations.

**Wordsong**
An imprint of Astra Books for Young Readers,
a division of Astra Publishing House
wordsongpoetry.com
**Printed in China**

ISBN: 978-1-63592-386-5 (hc)
ISBN: 978-1-63592-566-1 (eBook)
Library of Congress Control Number: 2021906400

**First edition**
10 9 8 7 6 5 4 3 2 1

Design by Barbara Grzeslo
The text is set in Frutiger Bold Condensed.
The illustrations are done using graphite sketches painted digitally.